Dedication

To all family, friends, and
colleagues; llama rescue
societies; and to all children
who wish for a pony.

MASCOT BOOKS

www.mascotbooks.com

Five Mile Charlie: A Special Pony for Carly

©2021 Kimberly Adams. All Rights Reserved. No part of this publication may be reproduced, stored in a retrieval system or transmitted in any form by any means electronic, mechanical, or photocopying, recording or otherwise without the permission of the author.

Second printing. This Mascot Books edition printed in 2021.

For more information, please contact:
Mascot Books
620 Herndon Parkway, Suite 320
Herndon, VA 20170
info@mascotbooks.com

Library of Congress Control Number: 2021901918

CPSIA Code: PRT0621B

ISBN-13: 978-1-64543-692-8

Printed in the United States

Five Mile Charlie
A Special Pony for Carly

Kimberly Adams

Illustrated by **David Gnass**

Follow your dreams and wishes. They come true for those who work hard for them. Believe in what you can do and don't forget to be kind along the way. Carly learns these things and Charlie does too.

Carly lived on a farm in Oklahoma called Five Mile Farm. Carly was little but strong, and she loved to work and play. Carly had a wiener dog named Okie and a Yorkie named Mollie. She also had a cat called Wally and a parrot named Annie. A Bluetick hound from a neighboring farm visited from time to time. Carly called her Blue. The one thing missing from Carly's life on the farm was a pony. She wanted a pony more than anything.

Spring on the farm brought the arrival of new things—flowers, birds, and bunnies. All kinds of baby animals basked in the warmth of the new season. It was a time for new life on the farm, including the honeybees.

Just over the mountain, in an old house in the valley, lived a magical hive of bees. Carly walked to the valley every day to talk to the bees and tell them her wishes.

Nora, the queen bee, was long and graceful, and honored by all of the bees. Queen Nora was kind and smart, but she had no room in her hive for slackers. All the bees in the hive had a role. The worker bees took care of the hive and searched for flowers to make honey. The scout bees told the worker bees where flowers could be found.

Queen Nora made wishes come true for those who sought her out. Her best friend was a scout bee named Journey. Queen Nora knew Carly wished for a pony, so she sent Journey off in search of a pony for Carly. Journey flew for miles. During her search, Journey saw Grumps, the coyote. *Ole Grumps,* thought Journey, *I don't know why he has to be so mean.*

Grumps lived over the mountain in a dreary cave. He was scraggly and smelly. He only had a few teeth. Grumps disliked everyone.

All of the animals on the farm were afraid of Grumps.

Grumps hid behind the trees and only came out at night after the sun went down at the farm.

Journey continued to fly and saw something in the distance. "I see a pony! I found a pony for Carly!" Journey flew back to the hive to tell the other bees and Queen Nora.

At the hive, Journey began to dance. Not just any dance, but a special waggle dance. Journey's special dance let Queen Nora and the worker bees know where to find the pony for Carly. Queen Nora, who rarely left the hive, flew away with Journey to meet the pony.

"There's the pony!" said
Journey as she and Queen
Nora landed on a fence post.

"Hmm, this pony looks different. No
matter, this pony will make Carly a
very happy little girl," said Queen Nora.

However, the pony looked different
for a very good reason...

"I'm no pony! My name is Charlie. I'm a llama."

Charlie was not a normal llama—oh no, not at all. Charlie was bright white in color with tons of fluffy, wool fur. Charlie had tall ears, a long nose, and wide blue eyes with long black eyelashes. He also had long legs with big, sharp hooves.

"Farmer Bud will not be happy if I leave," said Charlie. "But Farmer Bud is never home, and I really don't think he will miss me." With strength and courage, Charlie followed Queen Nora and Journey back to Five Mile Farm.

Carly woke the next morning. She rubbed her sleepy eyes and stepped outside. But what was in the meadow? Carly ran toward Charlie. Charlie bowed down with his long lashes covering his eyes.

"Where did you come from?" asked Carly.

Charlie responded, "My name is Charlie. I came here to be your pony, but I'm a llama."

"I think you are beautiful, Charlie!" exclaimed Carly excitedly.

Carly ran into the house. She knew Charlie must be hungry. Carly opened the refrigerator, but there was nothing except for some cheese. "Maybe Charlie will like it," guessed Carly.

"Cheese for Charlie," Annie squawked!

"Cheese, please," cried Okie and Mollie!

Charlie licked his lips and savored every bite of the delicious cheese. Charlie then had a cheese face. All the animals laughed at cheese-face Charlie. Charlie laughed too.

As Charlie settled into his new life on Five Mile Farm, he became known for taking care of the other animals in the meadow. He loved all of the baby animals and wanted them to feel safe. The baby cows romped and played with Charlie. The baby deer came out of the thick woods to play with him too. Oh Charlie, what a funny creature with a cheesy face!

One day, as the sun set at Five Mile Farm, Grumps lumbered out of his cave. Down the road he went to Five Mile Farm. The other animals saw Grumps and ran to Charlie in fear. "Don't be afraid," said Charlie. Charlie stomped his hooves as Grumps came closer with his few snaggle teeth showing.

Grumps gave Charlie a mean scowl. "I'll be back!" yelled Grumps, as he ran away.

The next morning, Carly picked an apple from a nearby tree. "Here, Charlie, try some apple with your cheese."

"Carly, we must find a way to help Grumps. He needs friends," said Charlie.

"Let's go to the library and study what coyotes like," said Carly.

Off went Carly and Charlie, with cheese on his face, on a five mile walk from Five Mile Farm to town. The worker bees had been listening. Queen Nora would help.

It was a sunny walk down the dirt road to town. The birds sang a cheerful song. The daffodils smiled. Blue led the way. "This is a very good day," said Carly.

"Indeed, it is," said Charlie.

Be kind, be brave, be strong, be bold.
The story of Five Mile Charlie will continue...

About the Author

Kimberly Adams is a practicing attorney in
McAlester, Oklahoma, and the Municipal Judge in
her hometown of Kiowa, Oklahoma. She earned
a Bachelor of Science degree from Oklahoma
Wesleyan University in 1997 and a Juris Doctorate
from the University of Oklahoma in December
2000. Kimberly resides in rural southeast Oklahoma
on her farm at Five Mile. The loss of her pet llama,
Charlie, inspired a children's book series, starting
with this first installment. Other publications include
works printed at West Publishing Company, through
her appellate practice as an attorney.

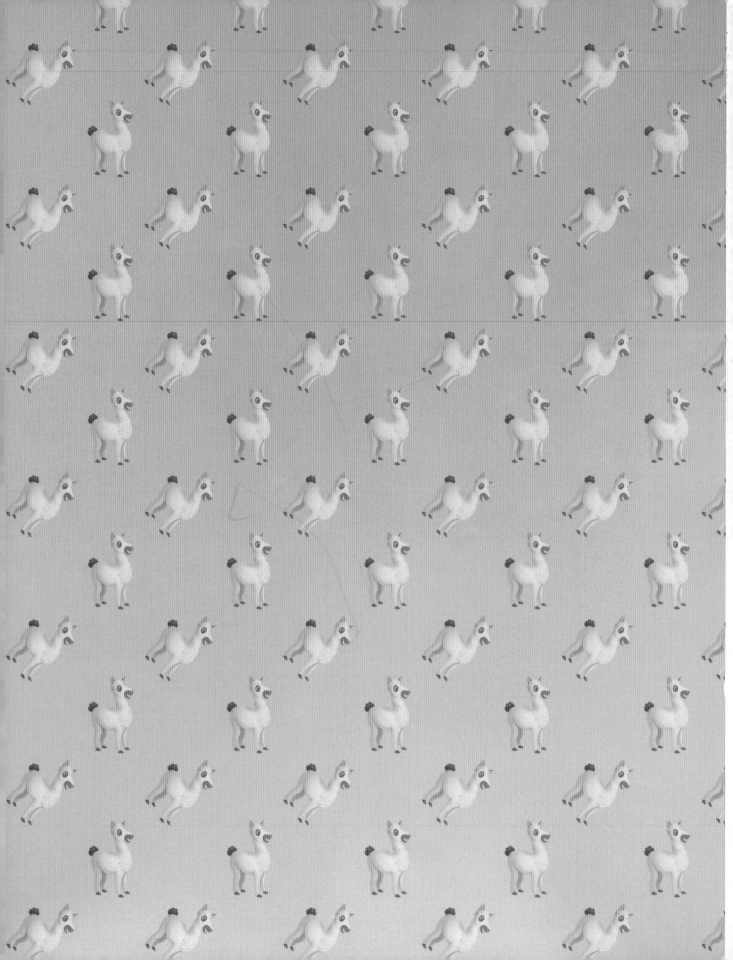